C000120946

TO Erin + Charlie

When you don't want to
walk, travel by leaf!
:)

Best wishes,
Annie + Laura

Levi Leaf Rider

Written by
Laura Jean Gannan

Illustrated by
Annie Dalton

Levi was a peculiar robin red breast

From the way he travelled,
to the way he dressed.

He wore goggles and wellies and
travelled by stream.

And for Levi this is the way it had always been.

For Levi travelled not by air but by leaf.

Which left the other
robins in disbelief.

See for Levi, he wanted to take it all in.

See each and every detail, on each and everything.

So, he whitewater rafted down fierce beautiful streams.

Watching the water drops forming like laser rainbow beams

Watching the way the water

Sprayed, SPLASHED and thrashed!

And often while wondering. He would very nearly CRASH!

He punted down brooks
taking it all in.

Whilst frequently playing his
miniature violin.

He watched the light changing in the trees.

The work done by those marvellous bees.

He sailed across shimmering lakes

Always being sure to bring his favourite fruit cake.

He would watch the animals on water, air and land.

Daydreaming about them all forming a band.

He surfed out to sea, using his wings
as sails to catch the maddest air.

He loved timing it for sunset to see
the sun's magnificent golden flair.

Watching dolphins perform, the waves were their stage.

Jumping, turning, playing! Regardless of their age.

And occasionally he would fly to see things from a different view.

But it always affirmed
what he already knew.

He was an original leaf rider
through and through.

A word from Levi

I choose to travel by leaf to take my time, to notice all of the tiny details,
the aroma of my surroundings and the sounds.

This way I can well and truly be in the moment.

I am not thinking about the past, as it has already happened. and I cannot change it.
I am not thinking about the future, as it has not happened yet.
I am enjoying the moment, each and every detail.

Some folk call this mindfulness, although this is not the only way to achieve mindfulness.

Drawing, colouring in, painting, exercise, dancing, cooking, craft, gardening,
playing a musical instrument, knitting and meditation are a few other ways I
observed others to achieve mindfulness.

Mindfulness is essential, as our brains are meaning making machines, constantly processing
and interpreting what is happening around us.

How our experiences impact us as an individual is unique, as not one person is
exactly the same: we are all different.

So allowing ourselves to slow down, and be in the moment allows our brain a chance
to rest a little, like a vacation from our busy meaning making brains.

For me, travelling by leaf is making the time to do this each day,
so I can have more brain space and resilience for life's challenges.

Mindful Nursery Rhymes

Levi Leaf Rider is accompanied by a nursery rhyme. You can find the tune on the
YouTube channel called, Mindful Nursery Rhymes

Levi's song is available for children, parents, careres & educators to enjoy
It helps us to check in with ourselves and our bodies.

When i am feeling in a spin and big feelings kick in
I try to slow down my mind
I look up at the trees and all the beautiful leaves
and I ask how am I ?
"I'm angry"
(breathe in, smell a flower, breathe out, blow out a candle)

When i am feeling in a spin and big feelings kick in
I try to slow down my mind
I look up at the trees and all the beautiful leaves
and I ask how am I ?
"I'm hungry"
(make munching sounds)

When i am feeling in a spin and big feelings kick in
I try to slow down my mind
I look up at the trees and all the beautiful leaves
and I ask how am I ?
"I'm thirsty"
(make drinking sound)

When i am feeling in a spin and big feelings kick in
I try to slow down my mind
I look up at the trees and all the beautiful leaves
and I ask how am I ?
"I'm tired"
(make snoring sound)